Base camp was buzzing with excitement! After months of planning for the volcanic expedition, the explorer was finally gathering his team together.

'We're going on a journey to find the jewels, my friends,' the explorer said. 'There are gemstones hidden in the rock at the top of the volcano.'

RUMBLE! RUMBLE! RUMBLE!

'Did you hear that?' a young miner asked,
feeling nervous. 'The volcano is waking up!'

'Actually, that was my stomach,' the other miner admitted.
The scientist reassured the team. 'I'll be monitoring the volcanic
activity so we aren't surprised by any sudden eruptions.'

The explorer continued, 'The scientist and the hungry miner will be the brains and stomach of the operation here at base camp. And you, young miner, will come with me to the top of the volcano to collect samples.'

The young miner drove the exploration truck to the top of the volcano. The brave explorer put on his heatproof suit and stepped out on to the cooled lava while the young miner looked on anxiously.

The explorer's eyes fixed on a lump of volcanic rock sticking out of the lava. 'This one looks like it will be full of gems!' he said, and set to work freeing it from the lava with his pickaxe.

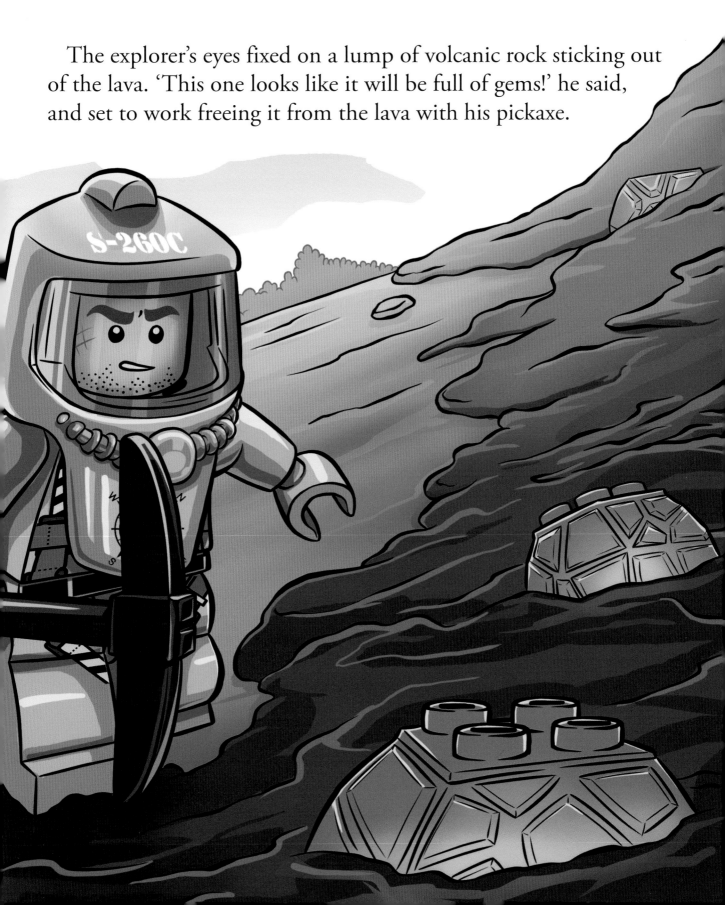

Back at base camp, the scientist monitored the volcano on her screen. All was quiet. The scientist smiled. 'Let's test the new drone.'

The hungry miner flew the drone over base camp.

The scientist was pleased. 'This will help us map the area to find jewels.'

Then the hungry miner flew the drone over to the lunch cart before landing it safely. 'It'll also help me see what's for lunch,' he thought. 'Mmm – sandwiches.'

Suddenly, the seismograph started juddering violently.

'Base camp to exploration truck,' the scientist radioed. 'We're seeing signs of possible tremors. You'd better get back, just in case.'

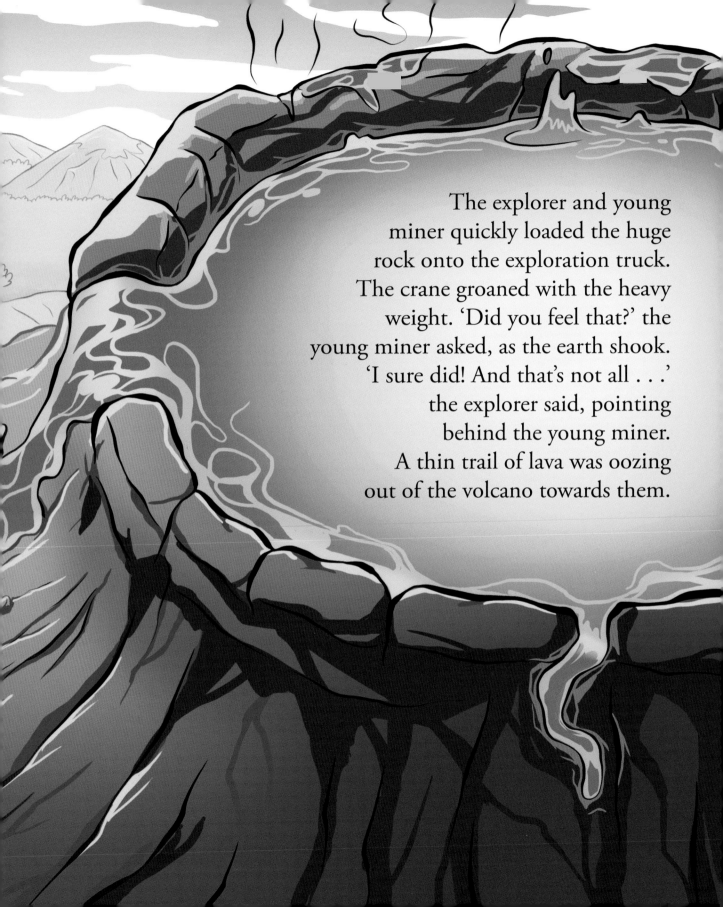

The explorer and young
miner quickly loaded the huge
rock onto the exploration truck.
The crane groaned with the heavy
weight. 'Did you feel that?' the
young miner asked, as the earth shook.
'I sure did! And that's not all . . .'
the explorer said, pointing
behind the young miner.
A thin trail of lava was oozing
out of the volcano towards them.

'Don't worry,' the explorer said to the young miner.
'This is normal for volcano expeditions. Let's check
in with the brains of the operation.'

The young miner nodded nervously.

'Exploration truck to base camp.' The explorer
radioed the scientist. 'We have a situation.'

'We can see,' the scientist replied. The lava was creeping closer. 'The lava is moving slowly, but volcanic activity is increasing.'

The young miner quickly started the exploration truck's engine.
VRRRMMMM!

'We need to rush, or we'll end up as lava mush,' the explorer said. The truck sped away from the volcano, carrying the precious cargo behind it.

The exploration truck soon arrived at base camp.

'How long until that lava stream reaches here?' the explorer asked the scientist.

'You mean how long until the *two* lava streams reach here,' the scientist replied, studying the satellite feed. Another lava stream had formed on the side of the volcano and was heading in the direction of the base.

'The lava is moving slowly,' the scientist reassured the team. 'But we should keep well away from it for today and come back when the activity has calmed down.'

The explorer agreed. 'We'll come back another day when the lava is at bay.'

'How will we know if we're safe from the lava as we travel home?' the young miner asked.

'We can use the drone as our eye in the sky!' the scientist exclaimed.

The scientist grabbed the drone and handed the
remote control to the hungry miner with a warning:
'It has heat protection, but the infrared camera will melt
if you fly it too close to the lava.'

'Drone lightly toasted, but not burnt. Got it,'
said the hungry miner, still thinking about food.
    The hungry miner launched the drone. It flew
through the air, scanning the area and showing the
team what its camera could see.

The team packed up their excavator, explorer truck, quad bike and research base.

The explorer looked at the lava rock sample and said, 'Whatever is inside you has waited a long time to be discovered. It can wait a little longer.'

The team started to make their way home. Watching the drone fly through the air, the scientist said, 'The drone's monitor is showing a large rock formation ahead.' She checked the lava flow. 'The lava is catching us up, but I don't think we can go over or around this wall of rock. So we'll have to go *through* it!'

When they reached the rock formation, the explorer got into the excavator. The way ahead looked completely blocked but the scientist told the explorer what to do. 'This is basic science – a steady force directed in one place will break the solid rock.'

The explorer agreed. 'This machine will do the trick but the lava's coming so I'd better be quick!'

The excavator steadily chipped away at the rock wall to open a path. The team was soon safely past the blockage.

'Well, at least we know our new equipment works. The drone was awesome!' the scientist said to the explorer. 'When the volcanic activity has calmed down, we can start again and collect more rocks.'

'We do have one sample,' the explorer replied, his eyes lighting up with excitement.

The explorer unloaded the rock sample and got into the excavator again. The drill began whirring. After a few minutes, there was a loud **_CRACK_**.

'Would you like to do the honours?'
the explorer asked the young miner.
    The young miner used his pickaxe to open
the rock. Inside were shiny, precious gemstones.

'Aren't you going to say something witty that rhymes?' asked the young miner.

The explorer thought for a moment, and then mumbled quietly to himself, 'This gemstone dream happened because we are a team?'

Marvelling at the glittering gems, the explorer simply added, 'Let's just say that good things come to those who wait.'

Just then, there was another rumble. It was the hungry miner's tummy again. 'Well, I don't think I can *wait* for lunch much longer!'

THE END